Grey Rabbit's Odd One

Alan Baker

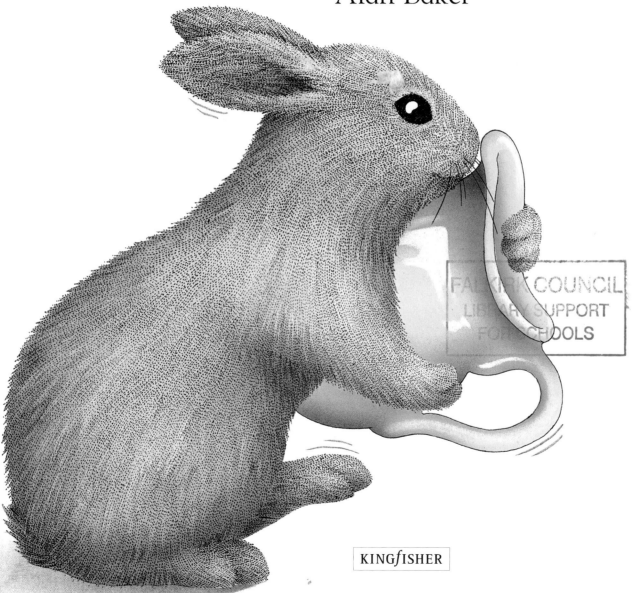

KING*f*ISHER

KINGFISHER
An imprint of Kingfisher Publications Plc
New Penderel House, 283-288 High Holborn
London WC1V 7HZ

First published in paperback by Kingfisher 1995
This edition published in 1998
4 6 8 10 9 7 5 3
3 (3TR)/0199/TWP/PW/NYM 170

Originally published in hardback by Kingfisher 1994

Copyright © Alan Baker 1994

A CIP catalogue record for this book
is available from the British Library

ISBN 1 85697 403 0

Printed in Singapore

One morning Grey Rabbit could
not find his favourite book.
What a mess!

It's time to tidy up, thought Rabbit.
First let's sort the wooden animals.

There were two of each kind just like in Noah's Ark.

But one thing was not an animal.
What was the odd one out?

A teaspoon.

So Rabbit tidied his tea-set.
But one thing did not belong.
What was it?

A paintbrush.

Rabbit gathered up his paints and brushes and made a useful sign. Now what was the odd one out?

A red and yellow spotted ball.

Rabbit found all his round things.
Hey, stop rolling away!
But one thing did not belong.
What was it?

A purple vase.
Where can that go? thought Rabbit.
It's the only vase I have.

Then he matched it up with all the other purple things. But something wasn't purple. What was it?

A duck. That belonged with the other soft toys so Rabbit lined them all up in a row.

Now what did not belong?

A brick.

There were lots and lots of bricks.
How could Rabbit sort them out?

First he built a block
of red bricks,

then a wall
of green bricks.

The yellow bricks made a tower.
What was that among the blue bricks?

Look! Rabbit's favourite book.
I'll tidy the blue bricks,
he thought, then read
my story.

At last!